♡ TACT ♡ ♡ EMPATHY

CONSIDERATION

CARE ♡

♡

GENEROSITY

♡ TOLERANCE

GRACIOUSNESS ♡

♡ HELPFULNESS

THOUGHTFULNESS ♡

A World of Kindness

From the EDITORS & ILLUSTRATORS of PAJAMA PRESS

THIS BOOK BEGAN when my three-year-old granddaughter Alice started pre-school and experienced a little unkindness from a fellow student. Her supportive mom reassured Alice that being kind was the best solution, which prompted Alice to ask me, "Nana, how can I be kind?" So we explored some of the many ways we can be gracious to others and how simple, thoughtful acts of kindness can become part of our everyday lives. Listening to Alice, I knew right away that here was a book I wanted to publish.

Our editors at Pajama Press eagerly embraced the challenge. We worked together to create a unique book that would spur conversations about how to be considerate of each other. Ann Featherstone, our Senior Editor, polished the text. I reached out to many of our illustrators to see if they would be interested in collaborating on this special project. I felt that each illustrator could approach the text with sensitivity and in their own style, allowing every spread to tell its own story. The unanimous response from our artists was so passionate that I knew we were onto something powerful.

What has been most rewarding for Pajama Press has been the overwhelmingly positive response we've received to this picture book. Our decision, therefore, to donate the royalties to the organization Think Kindness just seemed like the natural thing to do: a way for us to continue the book's impact.

We hope that *A World of Kindness* will inspire you to talk with the children in your life about kindness and how important it is in our uncertain world.

With kindness,

Gail Winskill, Publisher
Pajama Press

TABLE OF CONTENTS

The original cover art was created and donated by
award-winning author-illustrator Suzanne Del Rizzo

ARE YOU KIND?

Do you **wait**
your turn?

Will you **help** someone **younger**…

...or **older**?

Are you **gentle**
with animals **big**…

...and **small**?

Do you say **please** and **thank you**?
It's easy, you know.

But…can you say
"I'm sorry" if ever you're wrong?

Could you **share** something **special**?

When someone is shy, do you **help** her **join** in?

Will you **watch over** someone else?

When someone is sad, will you
comfort him?

Will you be a **friend** to someone **new**?

And that, my friend, is how
a **little kindness** grows into
a **world of kindness**.

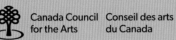

The publisher gratefully acknowledges the support of the Canada Council for the Arts and the Ontario Arts Council for its publishing program. We acknowledge the financial support of the Government of Canada through the Canada Book Fund (CBF) for our publishing activities.

Library and Archives Canada Cataloguing in Publication

A world of kindness / from the editors & illustrators of Pajama Press.

ISBN 978-1-77278-050-5 (hardcover)

1. Kindness--Pictorial works--Juvenile literature. 2. Children--Conduct of life--Pictorial works--Juvenile literature. 3. Kindness--Juvenile literature. 4. Children--Conduct of life--Juvenile literature. I. Pajama Press, issuing body

BJ1533.K5W67 2018   j177'.7   C2018-902618-9

Publisher Cataloging-in-Publication Data (U.S.)

Names: Featherstone, Ann, editor. | Anderson, Tara, illustrator. | Bender, Rebecca, 1980-, illustrator. | Deines, Brian, illustrator [and 6 others]
Title: A World of Kindness / from the editors & illustrators of Pajama Press.
Description: Toronto, Ontario Canada : Pajama Press, 2018. | Summary: "Nine celebrated children's picture book illustrators, including Rebecca Bender, Wallace Edwards, and Suzanne Del Rizzo, unite to illustrate an empowering text that celebrates, in a series of questions, the ways young children can show kindness. All royalties will be donated to Think Kindness"— Provided by publisher.
Identifiers: ISBN 978-1-77278-050-5 (hardcover)
Subjects: LCSH: Kindness – Juvenile fiction. | Friendship – Juvenile fiction. | Courtesy – Juvenile fiction. | BISAC: JUVENILE FICTION / Social Themes / Emotions & Feelings. | JUVENILE FICTION / Social Themes / Values & Virtues.
Classification: LCC PZ7.F438Wo |DDC [E] – dc23

Cover and book design by Rebecca Bender

Manufactured by Qualibre Inc./Print Plus
Printed in China

Pajama Press Inc.
181 Carlaw Ave. Suite 251 Toronto, Ontario Canada, M4M 2S1

Distributed in Canada by UTP Distribution
5201 Dufferin Street Toronto, Ontario Canada, M3H 5T8

Distributed in the U.S. by Ingram Publisher Services
1 Ingram Blvd. La Vergne, TN 37086, USA

COMPASSION ♡

♡ PATIENCE

♡ SYMPATHY

♡

UNDERSTANDING

♡ FRIENDLINESS

♡

♡ HONESTY

GENTLENESS ♡